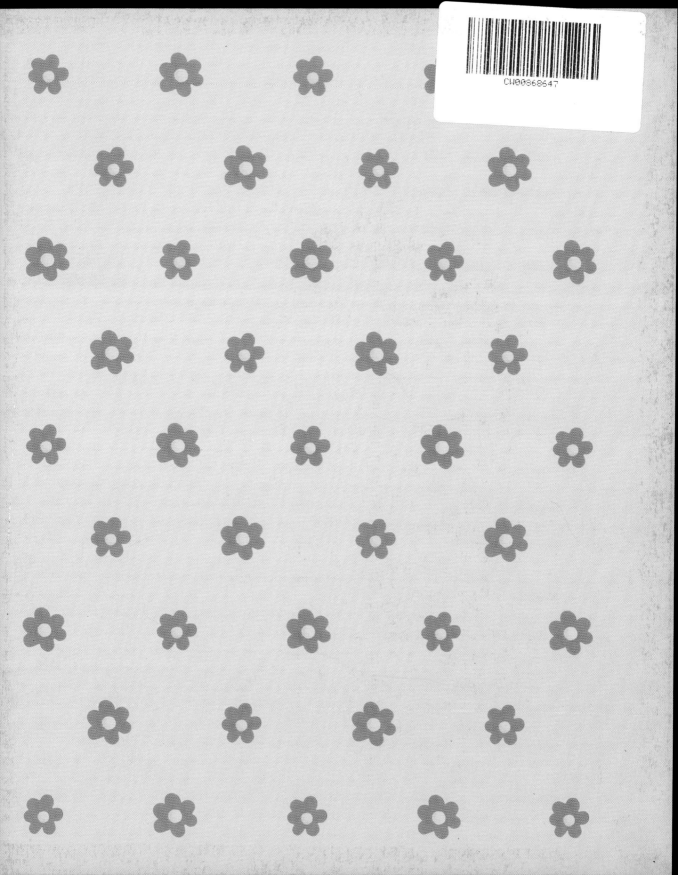

© 2004 Bookmart Limited

Published by
Armadillo Books
an imprint of
Bookmart Limited
Registered Number 2372865
Trading as Bookmart Limited
Blaby Road
Wigston
Leicestershire LE18 4SE

ISBN 1-84322-285-X

10 9 8 7 6 5 4 3 2

Produced for
Bookmart Limited by
Nicola Baxter
PO Box 215,
Framingham Earl
Norwich NR14 7UR

Designer: Amanda Hawkes
Production designer: Amy Barton

Printed in China

Starting to read – it's perfect!

The not-so-perfect baby in this story helps to make
sharing books at home successful and enjoyable.
The book can be used in several ways to help
beginning readers gain confidence.

You could start by reading the illustrated words
at the edge of each lefthand page with your
child. Have fun trying to spot the same words in
the story itself.

All the words on the righthand page have already
been met on the facing page. Help your child to
read these by pointing out words and groups of
words already met.

Finally, all the illustrated words can be found
at the end of the book. Enjoy checking all the
words you can both read!

The not so Perfect Baby

Written by Nicola Baxter · Illustrated by Pauline Siewert

ARMADILLO

girl

mum

bed

baby

This story is about a little girl called Anna-Mae.

One night, Anna-Mae's mum tucks her into bed and gives her a big hug.

"Anna-Mae," she says, "I want to tell you something. You are going to have a baby brother or sister."

"I want a baby sister!" says Anna-Mae.

cot

curtains

cupboard

toys

Next day, Anna-Mae asks, "Where will the baby sleep?"

"In the spare room," says Mum. "We will get a cot and some new curtains and a cupboard for the baby's toys."

"The baby can have some of my toys," says Anna-Mae.

She goes to her bedroom.

Anna-Mae goes to get some toys.

book

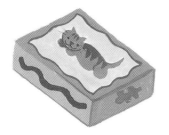

jigsaw

crayons

hoop

Anna-Mae finds a book about fairies...

and a jigsaw...

and some crayons...

and a hoop.

"These are for the baby," she says. "From me."

"Oh no," says her mum. "A baby can't play with those. When they are little, babies can't do very much."

"Can't the baby play with **me**?"
asks Anna-Mae.

coffee

biscuits

juice

milk

Mum has a good idea.

"I will ask my friend Rosie and her baby to visit," she says, "so you can see what babies are like."

Rosie's baby is called Ben.

Rosie and Mum have coffee and biscuits.

Anna-Mae has juice and biscuits.

Ben just has milk.

"I'm afraid he isn't much fun for you," Rosie tells Anna-Mae.

"What a good baby he is!"
says Mum.

fingers

toes

paints

nose

"I love all babies,"
says Anna-Mae.

"They have perfect little fingers
and perfect little toes.
And they smell lovely."

But Ben puts his fingers in
Anna-Mae's paints.

He kicks with his toes at
Anna-Mae's nose!

And he is awfully smelly!

Baby Ben is not perfect at all!

door

Mum and Anna-Mae wave goodbye to Rosie and Ben.

Mum shuts the door.

dad

"Mum," says Anna-Mae, "I don't want a brother or a sister after all."

"It's too late," smiles Mum. "Your baby is going to be here soon!"

school

The next day, Anna-Mae's dad is there to meet her at the end of school.

car

"Get in the car, darling," he says. "I've got a surprise for you."

"We are going to meet your sister!"
says Dad.

chair

mouth

eyes

sleepsuit

Mum is sitting in a chair.

"Would you like to hold your new sister, Anna-Mae?" she asks.

"Will she kick my nose, do you think?" asks Anna-Mae.

"Maybe," says Mum, "but she will love you."

The baby is warm.
She has a little pink mouth and big blue eyes.
She is wearing a pink sleepsuit.

The baby squeezes Anna-Mae's finger and goes to sleep.

"Oh, I do love my new sister,"
says Anna-Mae.

Picture dictionary

Now you can read these words!

bed

biscuits

book

car

chair

coffee

cot

crayons

cupboard

curtains

dad

door

eyes

fingers

girl

hoop

jigsaw

juice

milk

mouth

mum

nose

paints

school

sleepsuit

toes

toys